Knowing Wukong

Understand *Black Myth: Wukong*'s original story: *Journey to the West*

Table of Contents

Preface

Welcome to the extraordinary world of *Journey to the West*, a timeless Chinese literary classic that has captivated imaginations for centuries. As you embark on this literary odyssey, you are preparing to traverse a realm filled with mythical beings, epic adventures, and profound lessons that have transcended cultural boundaries.

Journey to the West, attributed to Wu Cheng'en, is a masterpiece that weaves a tapestry of fantastical tales inspired by the pilgrimage of the Buddhist monk Xuanzang to India. At its core is the indomitable Monkey King, Sun Wukong, a character whose charisma, wit, and powerful abilities have made him an icon in global storytelling.

In the midst of this rich tapestry emerges **_Black Myth: Wukong_**, a video game that breathes new life into the age-old tale. Game Science Studio, a visionary game developer, has undertaken the ambitious task of bringing the Monkey King's adventures to life in a stunningly immersive experience. As we delve into the intricacies of Black Myth: Wukong, it becomes paramount to understand the literary roots from which this gaming marvel springs.

This book serves as a gateway, bridging the East and West, to ensure that the Western audience can fully appreciate the cultural and mythological depth that Journey to the West offers. From the trials and tribulations faced by the pilgrims – Tripitaka, Monkey, Pigsy, and Sandy – to encounters with demons, deities, and dragons, each chapter of this epic tale enriches the narrative tapestry.

Join us on a journey through the pages of this timeless classic, and as you turn each leaf, envision the landscapes that Black Myth: Wukong seeks to reimagine. Gain insights into the characters, the moral lessons embedded in the narrative, and the cultural context that has made Journey to the West an enduring masterpiece.

Whether you are a seasoned scholar of world literature or a newcomer to the fantastical realms of Sun Wukong, let this book be your guide. Together, let us embark on a quest that transcends time and culture, unlocking the gates to the magical world of Journey to the West and paving the way for a deeper understanding of Black Myth: Wukong. May the journey be as enlightening as it is enchanting.

Introduction

China has a long and esteemed literary history stretching over 3,000 years, rooted in works like the Classic of Poetry dating back to 1000 BCE. Storytelling has always been an essential part of Chinese culture for exploring history, values, philosophy and also religion.

Journey to the West emerged from a rich tradition of Chinese mythology filled with legendary gods, legendary creatures, mystical lands, and stories passed down through oral and written works over millennia. Works like Classic of Mountains and Seas compiled myths and tales as early as 4th century BCE. Gods of nature, the cosmos, seasons as well as legendary rulers and heroes were venerated.

Chinese mythology dragons

Many myths included visits to divine immortals and paradises in the mountains. The gods were thought to influence events and dictated order over spiritual and earthly realms. These myths constituted an early form of religion in China that would later develop into structured belief systems like Daoism, Buddhism and folk religions.

Buddha statue

Pilgrimages to holy mountains and stories of journeys featured prominently in myths and spiritual lore. The heroes in these stories faced dangers like mischievous spirits, monsters and bandits. The journeys served as allegories for the spiritual enlightenment the travelers sought, influenced by religious teachings of Daoism and eventually Buddhism that journeyed to China from India.

These pilgrimages persist both in myths as well as records of actual monks traveling great distances to bring back scriptures and teachings to China. The story of Xuanzang's (玄奘) epic pilgrimage to India became legendary. The mythological novel Journey to the West applies layers of magical realism onto this historical record by incorporating beloved folk tales and myths into a unified epic novel.

Journey to the West is one of the Four Great Classical Novels of Chinese literature, having a profound impact on Chinese culture and language over the last 450 years since its publication. The tale draws heavily from factual records as well as legends surrounding the actual 7th century monk Xuanzang and his epic pilgrimage to India.

Xuanzang is a revered and almost mythical figure in China, credited for establishing direct contact between China and India and bringing Buddhist scriptures, ideas and culture into China during the Tang dynasty. He trekked to India in 629 CE, studying in many places before returning 17 years later, believed to have brought over 600 texts back to China.

His arduous and momentous journey along the Silk Road left a deep impression in literature and oral tales. The myths surrounding demons and dangers facing him grew more fantastical, on top of the already significant natural perils faced. He was said to have attained near supernatural feats.

When Wu Cheng'en (吴承恩) authored the 100-chapter novel in the 16th century Ming dynasty, seven centuries after Xuanzang's journey, he fused history with drama, magical realism with religious allegory, human struggle with spiritual enlightenment. The monk and his disciples would represent cornerstones of Buddhism - discipline, perseverance and wisdom triumphing over temptation, nature and evil. The tale invokes laughter as well as awe at spectacular battles, diabolical villains, mystical sages and improbable triumphs.

Beyond direct religious connections, the iconic character Monkey King also emerged as a cultural icon and shared symbol across Chinese communities. Journey to the West no doubt remains one of the most influential works of Asian literature as well as a treasured adventure tale for all.

Wu Cheng'en was born around 1500 CE near Shanghai during the Ming Dynasty in China. Not much is conclusively known about his personal life, but he is believed to have been a scholar, poet, and highly educated government functionary holding various local administrative roles.

Literary records suggest he authored Journey to the West in the latter half of the 1500s, completing the 100-chapter novel some time before his death around 1582. The novel is considered one of China's Four Great Classical Novels (the other three are *Water Margin*, *Romance of the Three Kingdoms*, and *Dream of the Red Chamber*) from that era.

Drawing from his classical education and Buddhist teachings, Wu Cheng'en infused history and legend surrounding the famous Tang dynasty monk Xuanzang with vivid imagination, humor and skillful storytelling. He built an epic adventure tale fusing real figures and supernatural beings interwoven with allegory and satire with profound cultural influence.

The novel reflects social commentary and Daoist skepticism paired with reverence for Xuanzang's dogged perseverance in seeking scriptures in India. Journey to the West evokes laughter while commending virtue and discipline against temptations of lust, greed, vanity, and ego. The universal theme of enlightenment's triumph over evil made it an enduring classic.

Wu Cheng'en's own life is shrouded in mystery with sparse verified details available. But through this epic novel Journey to the West, his creative vision and literary mastery earned immense acclaim in China as well as internationally over four and half centuries. The iconic Monkey King is his most famous creation, beloved for his defiant wit and resourcefulness.

Chapter 1: Origins of the Monkey King

The birth of Wukong

Sun Wukong (孙悟空), known as the Monkey King, was born from an enchanted stone egg that sat atop the Flower-Fruit Mountain, fertilized by the forces of Heaven and Earth over eons. The stone egg turned into a rock, then gained consciousness, hungrily observing the world around it.

On one stormy night, bolts of lightning struck the stone egg, causing it to crack open. A powerful monkey emerged, earning the name "Stone Monkey". He was hailed as a Messianic king by the monkey tribe for his uncanny abilities and took leadership.

Sun Wukong possessed immense strength, fiery golden eyes enabling him to recognize demons, and knowledge innately from birth. After spending over a decade enjoying games and pranks with his monkey tribe, one day Wukong realized all things fade away and die, pondering questions of mortality.

Achiving Immortality

Monkey goes off across the oceans to find a divine education

Seeking a sage to teach him immortality and detachment from temporal pleasures, Wukong wandered alone for 10 years across oceans and searched many mountains before finding the Sage Subhuti who taught him virtue, meditation, yin-yang philosophy and the secrets of infinity, granting him the religious name "Wukong", meaning "aware of emptiness".

Patriarch Subodhi transfers to Wukong the secret formulas of the immortals

Under the patient guidance of Patriarch Subhuti, Sun Wukong mastered multiple essential disciplines over several years. He gained skills in magical transformations, combat arts, meditation, yin-yang manipulation, herbal medicine preparation, and tested successfully in final exams on ethics and affinity.

His core magical skills included:

- 72 Earthly Transformations (qishi'er disha bianhua, 七十二地煞变化) allowing him to change into various animals, objects and forms.
- Somersault Cloud (jindou yun, 筋斗云) enabling him to travel vast distances in a single leap by conjuring a cloud.
- Various methods of locking and tracking demons using spells.
- Skills to raise demonic armies and spot disguises.

His martial talents encompassed:

- Expert staff fighting techniques with his Compliant Golden-Hooped Rod.
- Swordsmanship and blade arts.
- Wrestling and hand-to-hand combat methods.
- Throwing and striking with meteors through space manipulation.

He also learned Daoist practices for manipulating natural forces:

- Spells for elemental control over lightning, fire, storms.
- Mystical arts for healing and rejuvenation.

- Techniques for yin-yang disruption to confuse opponents.

Additionally, Wukong gained competence in Buddhist dharma knowledge, recitation, and mindfulness-cultivation through years of cleaning temples and attending scripture readings.

Also in the mystical depths of the underworld and Hell, Wukong becomes a tempest of chaos, unleashing havoc that reverberates through the ethereal realms. Standing before the sacred Register of Life and Death, he executes a daring rebellion by expunging his own name from the revered scroll. With a stroke of otherworldly audacity, Wukong ensures his soul remains untethered, free from the meticulous management of cosmic forces. This audacious act disrupts the orchestrated balance of existence, leaving an indelible mark on the cosmic narrative - an assertion of autonomy against the preordained dance of life and death.

Acquiring the Gold-Banded Staff

Recognizing the need for a formidable weapon, Wukong, with a strategic foresight, embarks on a quest to procure an extraordinary armament for himself. His destination is the abode of the Dragon King of the East Sea, a revered deity with access to powerful treasures.

Monkey King with Gold-Banded Staff

In a diplomatic exchange, Wukong seeks and obtains his primary weapon, the "Gold-Banded Staff of Miraculous Will" (ruyi jingu bang, 如意金箍棒). Crafted with celestial artistry, this staff becomes an extension of Wukong's formidable abilities, a symbol of both his martial prowess and his quest for enlightenment. With this newfound weapon in hand, Wukong is poised to face the challenges that lie ahead on his transcendent journey.

The Gold-Banded Staff of Miraculous Will is a magical and transformative weapon. This staff plays a significant role in the epic tale, showcasing both its incredible size and its ability to change in size at the will of its master.

Key features of the Gold-Banded Staff include:

- Size Manipulation: One of the most notable attributes of the staff is its capacity to change size. Sun Wukong can command it to extend or shrink, making it a versatile and powerful tool in various situations. In its compressed form, the staff can be carried easily, but when unleashed, it can reach colossal proportions, capable of reaching the depths of the ocean or stretching into the sky.
- Weight Control: Despite its massive size, the staff can be as light or as heavy as Sun Wukong desires. This allows him to wield it with ease in combat, performing incredible feats with agility and precision.
- Indestructibility: The staff is virtually indestructible. It can withstand powerful attacks and remains impervious to damage. This durability adds to the Monkey King's formidable combat abilities.
- Symbolic Significance: Beyond its physical properties, the Gold-Banded Staff holds symbolic significance. It represents the disciplined will of its master, reflecting Sun

Wukong's determination, strength, and control over supernatural forces.

The Gold-Banded Staff is not merely a weapon; it becomes an extension of Sun Wukong's character and a symbol of his might. Its magical properties contribute to the Monkey King's prowess, making him a formidable force as he embarks on his journey to retrieve the sacred Buddhist scriptures.

Wukong's aggregate abilities made him essentially undefeatable in single combat and allowed him to raise armies of beasts through magic spells and control mechanisms. But he would need to temper his impulsive arrogance before completing the journey to India.

Amnesty and Defiance against Heaven

The Jade Emperor

It turned out the Dragon Kings and Kings of Hell swiftly relay Wukong's audacious deeds to the Jade Emperor (yudi, 玉帝). Recognizing the need to keep a vigilant eye on the unpredictable Monkey, Venus the Metal Star (taibai Jinxing, 太白金星) extends an invitation for him to reside in Heaven, a strategic move to preempt any potential future disturbances.

In Heaven, Monkey's initial appointment as a horse-keeper with the title "Bimawen" (弼马温) incites his ire upon discovering his seemingly lowly rank.

Fueled by discontent, he defiantly returns to Flower-Fruit Mountain, self-proclaiming the lofty title of "Great Sage Equalling Heaven" (qitian dasheng, 齐天大圣), challenging the celestial hierarchy.

The Pagoda-Bearing Heavenly King Li (tuota li tianwang, 托塔李天上) leads a celestial army to apprehend Monkey in response to his rebellion. Undaunted, Monkey showcases his unparalleled prowess by defeating the elite celestial warriors, including the formidable Mighty-Spirit God (juling shen, 巨灵神) and Prince Nezha (哪吒).

Wukong duels Prince Nezha in the first war against Heaven

Undeterred by the initial defeat, the Jade Emperor dispatches Venus once again to extend an invitation to Monkey, this time conferring upon him the prestigious title of "Great Sage Equalling Heaven."

Assuming his role, Monkey is entrusted with guarding the Immortality-Peach Garden (pantao yuan, 蟠桃园). However, Wukong's innate mischievous nature compels him to indulge in the tempting peaches, consuming them voraciously. Learning of an unissued invitation to the upcoming

Immortality-Peach Banquet, Monkey, incensed, crashes the event prematurely. Unapologetically devouring all the food, imperial wine, and golden elixir of immortality, he unwittingly commits a grave transgression before realizing his error and retreating to Flower-Fruit Mountain.

In response to Monkey's flagrant defiance, the infuriated Jade Emperor marshals a formidable force of 100,000 celestial warriors to apprehend him. Undeterred, Wukong, displaying his unmatched prowess, single-handedly routs the celestial army, compelling their withdrawal. The celestial realms are left in awe of Monkey's indomitable spirit and unmatched martial skill.

Wukong fights the celestial army

However the Jade Emperor appeals to Buddha, who appears manifesting a giant palm that Monkey tries to somersault out of by magic cloud but fails - unable to escape the Buddha's grasp.

Punished by the Buddha

As punishment for his arrogant crimes and violence, the Buddha arranges Sun Wukong to be sealed under the Five Elements Mountain, his hands and feet pinned by a powerful talisman. There the Monkey King remains imprisoned for 500 years, regretting his rebellion and developing a willingness to serve penance for past wrongs when eventually released.

While causing great chaos through the heavenly palace, Wukong had drunk the sacred elixirs of immortality, eaten the peaches of heaven, appropriated a suit of golden armor, claimed victory over the dragon lords and demon kings across the lands. But he could not overcome the cosmic order upheld by the Buddha through the palm's crushing weight of his misdeeds.

Some legends say that under the mountain Wukong perfected his physical and mental powers - able to perceive all creation through senses honed to a razor's edge and halt emotion or sensation for seasons, emerging mightier for the ordeal with expanded insight on attaining release from endless striving and needing recognition.

Chapter 2: The Quest Begins

Chen Guangrui (陈光蕊), a renowned national academic champion, unfolds against a backdrop of love, tragedy, and the enduring spirit of retribution. His union with Yin Wenjiao (殷温娇) marks the beginning of a fateful journey that transcends both life and death.

As Chen embarks on a boat trip to assume his official post, the nefarious hand of bandit Liu Hong snuffs out his promising life, leaving Yin kidnapped and forced into a grim marriage. Undeterred by the shadows that darken her path, Yin later gives birth to Chen's son, a symbol of their love. Fearing for the child's safety, she sends him adrift in a basket down a winding river, accompanied by a poignant letter detailing her tragic tale.

Fortune, veiled in the mysterious workings of destiny, intervenes as the baby is discovered by the compassionate priests of a Buddhist temple. Embraced by the sanctity of the temple walls, the child is raised as a monk and bestowed the name Xuanzang (玄奘). Unaware of his noble lineage, Xuanzang grows, nurtured by the temple's teachings.

The veil of ignorance lifts as Xuanzang matures, revealing the harsh truth of his parents' fate. Fueled by a vow of vengeance, he channels his grief into action, filing an imperial report that leads to the arrest and execution of Liu Hong. In a symbolic gesture of justice, Liu's heart is offered as a sacrificial item for Xuanzang's deceased father, a poignant act of closure.

With the haunting echoes of his past guiding him, Xuanzang returns to life as a devoted Buddhist monk. Emperor Taizong, recognizing his courage and determination, sets the stage for a Grand Mass to promote Buddhism and release the souls of those who suffered wrongful deaths. Xuanzang is chosen as the head priest, a role that aligns with his destiny and purpose.

Guanying statue

Amidst the spiritual ceremonies in Chang'an, the arrival of Bodhisattva Guanyin introduces a celestial element to the unfolding narrative. Disguised as monks selling a cassock and priestly staff, Guanyin and her disciple, Hui'an, cross paths with Xuanzang. In a gesture of divine benevolence, Guanyin gifts the items to Xuanzang and unveils a greater purpose—the retrieval of true sutras hidden at Spirit Mountain.

With courage and determination etched in his heart, Xuanzang volunteers for the journey. In a testament to their shared purpose, Emperor Taizong swears brotherhood with him, and Xuanzang takes on the name Tripitaka Tang (唐三藏). As he sets forth from Chang'an, the sun dips below the horizon, marking the commencement of Tripitaka's epic journey to the west—a quest fueled by love, justice, and the unwavering pursuit of spiritual truth.

Tripitaka and Taizong become sworn brothers

In an ominous twist of fate, Tripitaka and the companions dispatched by the emperor find themselves ensnared in a cunning trap—a pit at Double-Fork Ridge, strategically designed to

31

capture unsuspecting travelers. Their predicament takes a dark turn as three formidable demon kings—an ominous trio comprised of a tiger, a bear, and an ox—seize control over their captured prey.

The dire situation escalates further as the demons, driven by their malevolent appetites, mercilessly cook and devour Tripitaka's two companions. A haunting silence descends as the demons, satiated momentarily, leave Tripitaka to await a similarly grisly fate in the shadows—a morbid promise of another meal to come.

In the midst of this peril, a sudden ray of hope emerges as Venus the Metal Star materializes. With grace and divine intervention, Venus guides Tripitaka out of the demons' lair, rescuing him from the clutches of impending doom. In a reassuring moment, Venus pledges to aid Tripitaka in recruiting powerful disciples who will serve as stalwart protectors on his arduous journey. The celestial promise of formidable allies imbues Tripitaka with renewed hope and determination as he embarks on the path ahead, guided by the cosmic forces that have intervened on his behalf.

Tripitaka journeyed on. When Tripitaka located the howling cave below the Five-Elements Mountain, the Monkey King told him of the wager with

Buddha that had trapped him there. By asking Tripitaka to lift the sealing talisman as a show of faith despite his daunting appearance, the monk freed the Monkey King after 500 years of remorseful anguish.

Sun Wukong found he could not escape the mountain's pull even unpinned until Tripitaka shared some words about mercy and virtue that helped correct the last of his spiritual ignorance imparted while helping him stand.

Overcome with gratitude and perceiving Tripitaka had an inner holy light, Monkey King weepingly bowed asking to serve as his humble disciple. He accepted the Buddhist name "Pilgrim Sun" and promised to sincerely guard Tripitaka with his life on the long journey to redeem past sins through this act of devotion.

Tripitaka then permitted him to become the first disciple, not knowing he had liberated the unruly Great Sage Equaling Heaven now eternally bound by loyalty and the power of the golden fillet to obey the priest as his new master.

After the first disciple Wukong killed some bandits, Tripitaka lectured him on showing compassion before a disgruntled Monkey King stormed off.

Appearing soon after, the Planet Venus told him not to worry and they would soon recruit three more disciples - Pigsy, Sandy and even a Dragon Prince transformed into a horse.

First, At the foreboding Eagle-Grief Stream (Yingchou Jian, 鹰愁涧), an unexpected challenge befalls Tripitaka as a dragon materializes and, with a swift motion, devours his white horse. Determined to retrieve the stolen steed, Monkey confronts the elusive dragon in a fierce battle that unfolds with relentless intensity. The dragon, however, proves to be a master of evasion, repeatedly vanishing into the stream, eluding Monkey's every attack.

Amidst the chaos, the compassionate Bodhisattva Guanyin descends to the scene. With divine grace, Guanyin intervenes, bringing resolution to the tumultuous clash. In an act of transformation, the dragon undergoes a metamorphosis, emerging as the iconic White Dragon Horse (Bai Longma, 白龙马). Guanyin, in her wisdom, imparts a crucial revelation to Monkey—only a supernatural creature like the White Dragon Horse possesses the resilience required for the arduous journey west. A mere mortal horse would succumb to the perils of the quest, underscoring the necessity of this enchanted companion for Tripitaka's pilgrimage.

Then there was Pigsy, Zhu Bajie (猪八戒), initially a marshal of the heavenly navy exiled to the mortal world for flirting with the Goddess of the Moon. He reincarnated as a pig monster commanded by Guanyin to await the pilgrims to join them as redemption. Monkey King defeated Pigsy in battle who then surrendered and accepted discipline as the second disciple to control his lecherous tendencies on the journey.

Pigsy and Monkey in the middle of a duel

Next a river spirit fought them who turned out to be the third disciple Sandy, Sha Wujing (sha heshang, 沙和尚), punished as a sandy-haired demon for breaking a crystal dish in heaven. Also bidding his time to meet Tripitaka's party, Sandy became the most junior member but had great powers over water and used his water-parting physique to help the group cross perilous currents ahead.

With his three disciples gathered - Monkey King, Pigsy, Sandy - and the Dragon Horse prince to ride, Tripitaka prepared to departure. A local abbot provided the pilgrims shelter on the first leg of their long and perilous journey toward the Spirit Mountains in distant India where the true scriptures awaited them. Soon demonic forces would test them but the disciples felt spirited witnessing such unified support.

Chapter 3: Key Battles and Encounters

The momentous quest for holy scriptures from India meant Tang Monk Tripitaka and disciples would face 81 ordeals or tribulations along the treacherous way - one for each of the 9x9 grades of enlightenment in Buddhism. These took the form of treacherous rivers, animal demons, forces of nature and bandits.

Wukong fights demons

The first several tribulations involved subduing tigers, dragons, battling the infamous White Bone Demoness who repeatedly regenerated after being struck down, and defeating various animal kings and sorcerers like the infamous Bull Demon King and his son Red Boy whose elemental powers nearly destroyed Monkey King.

Later tribulations included facing the formidable Three Rhinoceros Demons who wielded lightning and fire, an evil star deity who unleashed armies of spectral warriors, the Six Eared Macaque who could mimic Monkey King in every way, deadly insect devils like Centipede and Spider spirits, and macabre forces like skeleton and vampire specters.

Each battle tested the four pilgrim's teamwork and individual strengths to the utmost. After each victory Tripitaka would heal any injuries by reciting scriptures and then name a geographical feature after the incident before continuing the arduous journey. Over three years they prevailed against 81 perilous encounters before finally approaching the Thunderclap Monastery in India. There were also some interesting and bizarre encounters in the long journey as well, such as Tripitaka's pregnancy and Wokong turned into a watermelon to defeat an enemy.

Defeating the Tiger Vanguard

Amidst the rugged terrain of Yellow-Wind Ridge (Huangfeng Ling, 黄风岭), the pilgrims find themselves facing an unexpected adversary—the formidable Tiger Vanguard (Hu Xianfeng, 虎先锋, confirmed as enemy in Black Myth: Wukong). The air crackles with tension as Monkey and Pigsy engage in a relentless battle against the Tiger, their every move echoing through the mountains.

Tiger Vanguard

As the skirmish unfolds, the Tiger Vanguard, recognizing the imminent threat, opts for a tactical retreat, disappearing into the labyrinthine landscape. Undeterred, Monkey and Pigsy, fueled by determination, embark on a relentless pursuit, the echoes of their footsteps resonating through the rocky expanse.

In a cunning turn of events, the Tiger Vanguard, displaying strategic acumen, concocts a deceptive plan. Shedding his skin as a decoy, the illusory form distracts Monkey and Pigsy, while the true embodiment of the Tiger slips away, executing a sinister plot to kidnap Tripitaka and present him to his king.

The realization of the ruse strikes Monkey and Pigsy with a jolt, as they discover their master's absence. A sense of urgency compels them to trace the elusive demon's lair, and with tenacity in their hearts, they confront the Tiger Vanguard once more. The battleground is set for a decisive duel, the clash of forces reverberating through the cavernous expanse.

This time, however, the Tiger Vanguard, burdened by the weight of the impending confrontation, struggles to maintain the upper hand. Faced with the relentless onslaught from Monkey and the formidable strikes of Pigsy's rake, the Tiger finds himself cornered, bereft of escape routes. In a moment of climactic intensity, Pigsy delivers a decisive strike with his rake, vanquishing the Tiger Vanguard with unparalleled precision.

The echoes of victory resound through the mountainous terrain as Monkey and Pigsy, triumphant yet vigilant, stand over the defeated Tiger Vanguard. The chapter at Yellow-Wind Ridge concludes, leaving the pilgrims with a renewed sense of unity and purpose as they continue their arduous journey to the west.

Defeating the Yellow-Robed Monster

In the relentless pursuit of Tripitaka's flesh, the Cadaver Demon, harboring a thirst for immortality, employs a cunning guise to deceive the unsuspecting pilgrims. Shapeshifting into a young lady, the demon approaches Tripitaka, aiming to ensnare him in her treacherous web. However, Wukong's extraordinary Fiery-Eyes and Golden-Pupils (huoyan jinjing, 火眼金睛) pierce through each illusion, and a fierce battle ensues. The demon, undeterred, repeats her deceptive transformations twice more, assuming the forms of an old woman and an old man, before meeting her demise on the third strike. Her true identity is unveiled as Lady White Bone (baigu furen, 白骨夫人).

Monkey proceeds to attack the White Bone Demon disguised as a young lady

In a surprising turn of events, Tripitaka, misinterpreting Monkey's actions, accuses him of unjustly murdering innocent beings. The master banishes Monkey with an official letter, severing their discipleship.

Returning to Flower-Fruit Mountain, Wukong confronts a band of hunters terrorizing his monkey brethren. Justice prevails as he dispatches the oppressors and ensures the safety of his fellow primates. Meanwhile, Pigsy, on an alms-begging journey, vanishes for an extended period, prompting Sandy to embark on a quest to locate him.

During their absence, Tripitaka takes a solitary stroll into the forest, discovering a golden pagoda in the distance. Unbeknownst to him, the pagoda conceals the lair of the Yellow-Robed Monster (huangpao guai, 黄袍怪) and his minions. Captured within, Tripitaka becomes entangled in a struggle against the insidious forces.

The Yellow-Robed Monster

Recognizing their master's disappearance, Pigsy and Sandy engage in a fierce battle against the Yellow-Robed Monster, whose claim of being the King's son-in-law clouds the truth. A princess, kidnapped by the demon, reveals her identity and pleads for help. With the conflict escalating, Pigsy returns to Flower-Fruit Mountain, leveraging a strategic half-truth to goad Monkey into joining the fray.

Enraged and fueled by Pigsy's fabricated tale, Monkey returns to confront the Yellow-Robed Monster. The ensuing battle sees Monkey assisting the princess in escaping from the demon's clutches. However, Yellow Robe, recognizing Wukong, engages in a duel before hastily retreating, leaving Monkey to ponder the true nature of this celestial being.

A revelation unfolds as Wukong ascends to Heaven and discovers that Yellow Robe is a celestial star constellation. Armed with newfound knowledge, Monkey escorts the rescued princess back to Precious-Image Kingdom. The master forgives the misguided accusations, and Monkey, once again accepted as a disciple, resumes his role in the sacred pilgrimage to the west. The narrative weaves a tapestry of trials and redemption, transcending earthly bounds and celestial realms alike.

Defeating the Red Boy

As the pilgrims approached Roaring Mountain, a distressing cry echoed through the air, drawing them towards a forest where they discovered a seemingly helpless boy tied to a tree. Monkey, ever astute to the ways of demons, suspected a trick and offered to carry the boy back to his home.

Seizing the opportunity, Wukong attempted to throw the demon child off a cliff when the others were out of sight. However, the cunning boy escaped, summoning a demonic wind that abducted Tripitaka to his mountain cave.

Gathering information from local deities, the disciples learned that the boy was Red Boy (hong hai'er, 红孩儿), son of the Bull Demon King (niu mowang, 牛魔王) and Princess Iron Fan (tieshan gongzhu, 铁扇公主). Monkey, pleased by the revelation, asserted his authority as Red Boy's uncle, owing to his sworn brotherhood with the Bull Demon King.

Demanding Tripitaka's release, Wukong and Pigsy engaged Red Boy in a fierce battle. The infant king displayed his formidable powers, blowing mouthfuls of the True Fire of Samadhi that forced Monkey and Pigsy to retreat.

Pigsy flees while Red Boy attacks Monkey with deadly Samadhi Fire

In a desperate bid for assistance, Monkey sought help from the dragon kings, but even their water reinforcements proved ineffective against the Samadhi Fire. Nearly succumbing to the smoke and flames, Monkey was saved when he fell into a stream and received a shock from the cold water.

Resuscitated by Pigsy, Wukong realized the need for divine intervention and instructed Pigsy to seek Guanyin's help. Meanwhile, Red Boy, in a mischievous move, sent minions to invite his father, the Bull Demon King, to feast on Tripitaka's flesh. Monkey, using his transformation skills, impersonated the Bull Demon King and gained access to the demons' cave.

Red Boy, growing suspicious, exposed Wukong's ruse and decided to invite Guanyin for assistance. Guanyin, ever resourceful, tricked Red Boy into sitting on her lotus platform, which transformed into a throne of swords, causing him great pain. Guanyin secured his surrender by placing five golden bands around his head, wrists, and feet, reciting a mantra that tightened the bands and brought Red Boy to submission.

With Red Boy subdued and his demonic antics quelled, the pilgrims could once again resume their journey, their encounter with the fiery trials of Roaring Mountain standing as a testament to the unpredictable challenges that lay ahead on the sacred path to the west.

Acrossing the Heaven-Reaching River

In the tranquil vicinity of Heaven-Reaching River (tongtian he, 通天河), a vast and insurmountable waterway, the pilgrims find refuge in a riverside village for a night of respite. Here, the villagers unravel the ominous tale of the Great King of Numinous Power (linggan dawang, 灵感大王), a formidable demon lord who aids the village in summoning rain. However, the demon's sinister appetite demands an annual sacrifice of a boy and girl, and this year, the unfortunate Chen family is slated for the ominous ritual.

Moved by compassion, Monkey and Pigsy volunteer to assist the villagers by infiltrating Numinous Power's temple. Transforming themselves into the sacrificial figures, the duo orchestrates a clever plot to apprehend the demon.

As the Great King of Numinous Power materializes for his customary feast, Monkey and Pigsy, hidden in plain sight, engage in a playful exchange with the demon before launching a surprise attack. Despite the demon's escape, two abandoned fish scales hint at a piscine origin, suggesting the demon to be a fish demon.

Numinous Power, now aware of Monkey's master and the potential for immortality through consuming Tripitaka's flesh, devises a cunning plan. Freezing the surface of Heaven-Reaching River, he creates a treacherous trap for the unsuspecting pilgrims. In a dramatic turn, Tripitaka falls through the ice and is captured, while Monkey, Pigsy, and Sandy narrowly evade capture.

Undeterred, Pigsy and Sandy plunge into the river, engaging Numinous Power in a fierce battle. luring the demon onto land, Monkey seizes the opportunity to confront him. The demon, terrified of Monkey's formidable powers, retreats back into the river, refusing to emerge again.

Facing a formidable adversary, Monkey seeks guidance from Guanyin, who reveals the surprising truth: Numinous Power is, in fact, her pet goldfish. Cultivating his powers by listening to Guanyin's Buddhist sutras, the goldfish transforms into a formidable demon. Guanyin intervenes by tossing a purple-bamboo basket into Heaven-Reaching River, subduing the demon.

In gratitude for ridding the river of the demon's menace, the benevolent Great White Turtle (dabai yuan, 大白鼋) offers to transport the pilgrims across the expansive river. Expressing his desire to attain human form, the turtle beseeches Tripitaka to seek guidance from the Buddha, marking a harmonious conclusion to their encounter with Numinous Power.

Ferried across the wide river by the Great White Turtle

Defeating the Princess Iron Fan and the Bull Demon King

As the pilgrims pressed on, a daunting obstacle loomed before them—the treacherous Mountain of Flames, its fiery peaks threatening to incinerate anything in their path. In a bid to secure safe passage, Monkey ventured to Princess Iron Fan's abode to borrow her coveted Plantain Fan, known for its ability to quell even the fieriest of flames.

However, the visit took an unexpected turn. Princess Iron Fan (tieshan gongzhu, 铁扇公主), grieving for the fate of her son Red Boy, held Monkey responsible and chose confrontation over cooperation. Using her formidable fan, she sent Monkey hurtling thousands of miles away.

Undeterred, Wukong swiftly returned, displaying his mastery of transformations by infiltrating Iron Fan's stomach. The discomfort forced the princess to yield the Plantain Fan, but slyly she handed over a counterfeit, setting the stage for Monkey's strategic ploy.

Princess Iron Fan with her powerful Plantain Fan

Undeterred by the fake fan's failure to subdue the Mountain of Flames, Wukong sought an alternative approach. Turning to Princess Iron Fan's husband, the Bull Demon King (niu mowang, 牛魔王), Monkey found himself embroiled in a fierce duel. The clash was interrupted by a messenger inviting the Bull Demon King to a party, allowing a temporary reprieve in their conflict.

Seizing the opportunity, Monkey cunningly stole the Bull Demon King's Water-Repelling Golden-

Eyed Beast and assumed the guise of the Bull to gain access to Iron Fan's residence.

Exploiting her belief that he was the real Bull Demon King, Wukong deceived her into surrendering the Plantain Fan—a second step in his elaborate plan.

The plot thickened when the real Bull Demon King discovered the theft. Transforming into Pigsy, Wukong unwittingly handed over the fan, leading to a climactic battle between the two powerful beings. Pigsy joined the fray, and reinforcements in the form of Heavenly King Li, Nezha, and celestial soldiers arrived to apprehend the Bull Demon.

After a prolonged and intense struggle, Bull and Iron Fan, realizing the futility of resistance, surrendered. The Plantain Fan, now in Wukong's possession for the third and final time, was wielded with magical prowess. With a mighty sweep, the flames of the Mountain of Flames were banished forever.

The pilgrims, now free from the fiery obstacle, could safely traverse the once-daunting Mountain of Flames. The triumph over this perilous trial marked a significant step forward in their epic journey to the west, where challenges and adventures continued to shape the destiny of the sacred quest.

Adventures in the Kingdom of Women

Amidst the exotic landscapes of the Kingdom of Women, Tripitaka and Pigsy unwittingly fall victim to the mystical Child-Mother River, a whimsical waterway that unexpectedly grants them pregnancies. In a peculiar turn of events, Monkey, their ever-resourceful guardian, is tasked with securing abortion water from the enigmatic True Immortal of Miracles (ruyi zhenxian, 如意真仙).

The True Immortal, recognizing Wukong as the conqueror of his nephew Red Boy (yes, he was another relative of the Red Boy), proves to be a formidable adversary. Refusing to relinquish the coveted abortion water, the Immortal employs cunning tactics to thwart Monkey at every turn. Undeterred, Monkey collaborates with Sandy to devise a clever plan, involving distraction and stealth, to acquire the essential liquid just in time to relieve his pregnant companions.

As the pilgrimage ventures further, the trio arrives at the captivating capital of the Kingdom of Women, where the Queen herself becomes enamored with Tripitaka and proposes marriage.

Swift-thinking Monkey orchestrates a strategic escape plan, advising Tripitaka to agree to the Queen's wishes to avoid potential repercussions.

Following an unconventional wedding feast, the Queen graciously certifies their passport, granting passage to Tripitaka's disciples. In a bittersweet farewell, Tripitaka and the Queen accompany the three pilgrims to the kingdom's border. Unexpectedly, a mysterious woman emerges, abducting Tripitaka and adding an unforeseen twist to their departure.

In a daring pursuit, Wukong infiltrates the demonic woman's mountain cave, witnessing his master's steadfast resistance against her seductive charms. A fierce battle ensues, culminating in a deadly sting from the demon's tail, afflicting both Monkey and Pigsy. Forced to retreat, the demon returns to her lair, continuing her attempts to ensnare Tripitaka.

Guided by Guanyin's counsel, Wukong seeks assistance from the Star Officer Krttika (maori xingguan, 昴日星官). The celestial being transforms into a giant rooster, unleashing a powerful crow that proves fatal to the demon. In her demise, the scorpion demon unveils her true identity, concluding another chapter in the epic journey.

Defeating the Spider Spirits and The Hundred-Eyed Demon

As the pilgrims continued their journey, Tripitaka, the venerable monk, went to beg for alms at a seemingly hospitable house. Unbeknownst to him, the house owners were not what they seemed—they were female demons, Spider Spirits (蜘蛛精), with sinister intentions, detaining Tripitaka with the aim of making him their next meal.

Wukong, ever watchful over his master, sensed trouble when Tripitaka didn't return. Seeking information from the local earth deity, Monkey discovered the true nature of the house owners and their dwelling at the Coiled-Silk Cave, where seven female demons resided.

Realizing the demons had gone to bathe at a nearby spring, Wukong entrusted the task to Pigsy, who, being tempted by the bathing women, attempted to join them. However, the demons, alarmed by his presence, shot silk threads from their bellies, entangling Pigsy in a sticky trap.

After the demons departed, Pigsy managed to free himself and rejoined Monkey and Sandy. The trio ventured to Coiled-Silk Cave, where Monkey swiftly defeated the minion guards and rescued Tripitaka from the clutches of the demons.

Enraged by their defeat, the seven demons sought refuge with their senior Daoist brother, informing him of their loss and imploring him to avenge them. When the pilgrims reached the Daoist's abbey, Monkey ruthlessly confronted the seven demon sisters, who, in their true forms, revealed themselves to be giant spiders. Despite their attempts to fight back, Monkey emerged victorious.

Hundred-Eyed Demon Lord

Faced with the wrath of the senior Daoist, Monkey engaged in a fierce battle. The Daoist, named the Hundred-Eyed Demon Lord (百眼魔君), with hundreds of eyes emitting beams of golden light, trapped Wukong within an unbreakable barrier. Near defeat and on the brink of death, Monkey received a timely revelation from a passing saint—a solution lay with Dame Pralamba.

Flying off to find Dame Pralamba, Monkey learned that only she possessed the means to break through the Daoist's golden beams. Pralamba, using a divine needle, halted the Daoist's onslaught. The Daoist's true form was revealed—a centipede demon. Tamed by Dame Pralamba, the demon was taken away, bringing an end to the threat posed by the Coiled-Silk Cave and marking another triumph on the pilgrims' arduous journey to the west.

Trapping in the Small Thunder-Clap Monastery

As the pilgrims continued their journey, the path led them to the serene grounds of the Small Thunder-Clap Monastery (xiao leiyinsi, 小雷音寺), nestled amidst ancient trees and mystical aura. Tripitaka, driven by his unwavering faith, insisted on paying homage to the Buddha within, despite Wokong's skeptical protests, who sensed an impending danger lurking within the temple's tranquility.

Small Thunder-Clap Monastery

Inside the temple, the atmosphere was peaceful, with an intricately crafted Buddha and his disciples adorning the sacred space. Oblivious to the impending peril, Tripitaka, Pigsy, and Sandy reverently knelt down to worship the Buddha. Monkey, however, detected a demonic presence in the seemingly divine figure. His instincts proved right when the demon king, Aged Buddha Yellow-Brows (huangmei laofo, 黄眉老佛), revealed himself and hurled a pair of golden cymbals.

61

The magical cymbals ensnared Monkey, rendering him captive while Tripitaka, Pigsy, and Sandy found themselves bound by mystical forces. The demon king, with a sinister grin, gloated over his captives. The situation seemed dire, but Monkey, ever resourceful, sought aid from the 28 Constellations (ershiba xingxiu, 二十八星宿). Through their combined strength, he managed to break free from the golden cymbals' grasp.

Undeterred, Yellow-Brows unleashed his Human-Seed Bag, a malevolent artifact capable of devouring beings into its ethereal depths. Monkey, determined to protect his companions, valiantly resisted but found himself sucked into the mysterious bag along with the 28 Constellations.

Inside the bag, Monkey strategized his escape, employing his cunning and resourcefulness. Utilizing the unique abilities of the 28 Constellations, he broke free from the confines of the Human-Seed Bag. Now liberated, Monkey sought aid from celestial warriors to confront the formidable Yellow-Brows.

However, Yellow-Brows, anticipating Monkey's move, swiftly detained the celestial warriors using his malevolent bag. Undeterred, Monkey continued his quest for allies and stumbled upon Buddha

Maitreya (mile fo, 弥勒佛), a benevolent force willing to assist him in subduing Yellow-Brows.

Buddha Maitreya revealed the dark past of Yellow-Brows, a former servant who betrayed his trust, stole treasures, and succumbed to demonic tendencies. Determined to rectify this betrayal, Maitreya offered his support to Monkey in bringing Yellow-Brows to justice.

Wokong, armed with this newfound alliance, devised a cunning plan. He lured Yellow-Brows into a watermelon field, where he transformed himself into a succulent watermelon. Once swallowed by the unsuspecting demon, Monkey unleashed his might from within, causing intense pain to Yellow-Brows. Overwhelmed by the agony, Yellow-Brows surrendered and submitted to Buddha Maitreya, marking the triumph of righteousness over demonic forces.

Defeating the Six-Eared Macaque

The journey takes an unexpected and dark twist as Tripitaka falls into the clutches of a gang of ruthless bandits. Bound to a tree, Tripitaka becomes the unwilling target of the bandits' malevolence. In a sudden surge of violence, Monkey, driven by an instinct to protect his master, dispatches two of the bandits with a lethal force. However, the consequences are swift and severe, as Tripitaka delivers a stern lecture to Monkey, reminding him of the sacred principles they must uphold.

Seeking refuge for the night, the pilgrims unwittingly find shelter at the home of an elderly couple, only to discover that the couple is the parents of one of the bandits. The revelation unfolds, painting a tragic picture of a rebellious and cruel son who inflicts harm even upon his own parents.

As the bandits catch sight of the pilgrims, a pursuit ensues, prompting Monkey to take drastic measures. With a decisive sweep of his staff, he confronts the bandits, culminating in the beheading of the unfilial son. The horrifying spectacle leaves Tripitaka appalled, leading him to recite the Tightening-Headband Mantra and banish Monkey from the group once again.

In his exile, Wukong seeks solace with Guanyin, who provides him with a temporary sanctuary. Meanwhile, Pigsy, tasked with a seemingly simple mission to collect water, succumbs to his usual slumber. Sandy leaves in search of both missing disciples, leaving Tripitaka vulnerable.

During their absence, another Monkey, bearing ill intentions, returns to assault Tripitaka and pilfer the pilgrims' luggage. Upon regaining consciousness, Tripitaka recounts the ordeal to his remaining disciples. Sandy, determined to rectify the situation, travels to Flower-Fruit Mountain to confront the impostor Monkey but is met with a formidable opponent he cannot overcome. The incident is reported to Guanyin, adding another layer of complexity to the unfolding saga.

At Guanyin's abode, Sandy discovers yet another Monkey, prompting him to inform Guanyin about the ongoing confusion. Together, Monkey and Sandy journey to Flower-Fruit Mountain to unravel the mystery surrounding the doppelgänger.

The confrontation between the real Wukong and his impostor intensifies into a prolonged and arduous duel. The battleground expands across Heaven and Earth, with their strength and abilities proving to be eerily identical. Even the discerning eyes of Guanyin, Tripitaka, and the formidable Demon-Reflecting Mirror fail to distinguish between them.

The real and fake Monkeys fight each other in a marvellous duel

Amidst the chaos, the creature Truth-Hearing from the underworld manages a partial revelation, then Tathagata Buddha identified the impostor as the Six-Eared Macaque. Frustrated by the confusion, Wukong takes matters into his own hands, slaying the Macaque before returning to Tripitaka. The journey, marred by betrayal and deception, continues with a sense of renewal and a deeper understanding of the challenges that lie ahead.

Chapter 4: Reaching the Destination

After an arduous and perilous journey, the pilgrims, led by the venerable Tripitaka, found themselves at the base of Spirit Mountain, the sacred abode of the Tathagata Buddha. The towering peaks seemed to reach into the heavens, shrouded in an ethereal mist that whispered tales of divine revelations.

To reach the Buddha's temple, the pilgrims faced the formidable challenge of crossing a mystical river. Undeterred, they boarded a seemingly bottomless boat that would ferry them across the ethereal waters to their destination. However, fate had other plans, as Tripitaka, the heart and soul of the pilgrimage, fell into the river during the treacherous journey.

A moment of despair turned into an unexpected revelation as Tripitaka was miraculously pulled back from the depths. The river had cleansed him of his mortal essence, bestowing upon him the gift of immortality. This divine transformation marked a turning point in the pilgrimage, elevating Tripitaka to a higher plane of existence, ready to face the challenges that lay ahead.

The pilgrims, now accompanied by their immortal leader, finally stood in the presence of the Tathagata Buddha. The air was charged with an otherworldly energy as they were escorted to the grand library of

Spirit Mountain. Here, the pilgrims were presented with what they believed to be the sacred sutras, a full set of scrolls that held the key to enlightenment.

The four pilgrims bow to the Buddha upon their arrival at Spirit Mountain

Their elation, however, was short-lived. As they were leaving Spirit Mountain, a mysterious hand descended from the heavens, tearing open the scrolls of sutras. To their dismay, the pilgrims discovered that the scrolls were wordless, devoid of the sacred teachings they had sought so diligently.

Feeling betrayed and deceived, the pilgrims returned to the Tathagata Buddha, demanding answers and the true sutras they had been promised. In the presence of the Buddha, their frustrations were laid bare, and the Tathagata, in his infinite wisdom, acknowledged their quest for the genuine scriptures.

With a solemn command, the true sutras were granted to the pilgrims, but not without a price. The Tathagata asked for their golden alms bowl as a token of gratitude. Reluctantly, the pilgrims handed over their cherished possession, recognizing the cost of the sacred knowledge they sought.

The golden alms bowl

The golden alms bowl, a symbol of their journey
and sacrifices, was offered as a humble tribute to
the Tathagata Buddha. With the authentic scriptures
in their possession, the pilgrims prepared to
continue their epic journey, armed not only with the
teachings that would guide them to the west but also
with the resilience forged through the trials at Spirit
Mountain. The path ahead was still uncertain, but
their unwavering determination and newfound
wisdom would propel them forward on the
pilgrimage of a lifetime.

As the pilgrims embarked on their journey back to the Tang Empire, carried by celestial clouds under the watchful gaze of Guanyin, a twist of fate redirected their course. The compassionate Bodhisattva, recognizing that they were one trial short of the sacred number of 81 tribulations, ordered the celestial escort to drop them off at Heaven-Reaching River.

Here, at the river's edge, they were met by the Great White Turtle, a venerable creature willing to aid them in crossing the wide expanse of water once again. However, the turtle, possessing ancient wisdom and a hint of impatience, posed a crucial question to Tripitaka.

In the midst of the river, the turtle asked Tripitaka whether he had inquired of Buddha whether he would attain human form. A moment of realization swept over Tripitaka as he confessed to forgetting this vital inquiry. The turtle, angered by this oversight, decided to teach them a lesson in humility.

With a swift and decisive motion, the Great White Turtle dunked the pilgrims into the river. The sacred scriptures, soaked and dripping, were in peril. Yet, the three disciples, ever vigilant and quick-witted, managed to rescue Tripitaka and salvage the precious sutras.

Now stranded on the riverbank, the pilgrims faced the challenge of drying the sacred scriptures. As the sutras lay spread out in the sun, the villagers from a nearby village, whom the pilgrims had once saved during their earlier journey to the Buddha, recognized their saviors.

The local villagers, grateful for the past assistance, welcomed the pilgrims into their midst. For the rest of the day, the travelers found refuge in the village, sharing stories of their adventures and basking in the warmth of the community they had once aided.

Amidst the laughter and camaraderie, the pilgrims reflected on the lessons learned at Heaven-Reaching River. The trials, though unexpected, served as a reminder of the importance of humility and diligence on their sacred quest. Little did they know that this unplanned detour would not only strengthen their resolve but also deepen the bonds between them as they prepared to face the challenges that still lay ahead on the journey to the west.

Conclusion

As the celestial clouds carried the pilgrims back towards Chang'an, the grand capital of the Tang Empire, anticipation and excitement filled the air.

The sprawling city soon came into view, its majestic towers and imperial palaces standing as a testament to the vibrant civilization that awaited them.

Emperor Taizong, aware of the triumphant return of the pilgrims, personally descended from his throne to welcome Tripitaka back to the capital. The entire palace grounds were alive with the rhythmic beats of drums, the melody of flutes, and the joyous cheers of the citizens. The emperor, with great respect and admiration, acknowledged Tripitaka's success in obtaining the sacred sutras.

Amidst the grand celebration, Tripitaka shared his remarkable experiences with his imperial brother. The emperor listened intently as the monk described the wonders and challenges encountered on the journey to the west. The tales of mythical beings, divine interventions, and the ultimate triumph over tribulations captivated the emperor's imagination.

The pilgrims were treated like honored guests in the imperial palace, indulging in sumptuous feasts and luxuriating in the comfort of their surroundings. The palace became a temporary haven, offering respite and celebration for the weary travelers who had endured countless trials in their quest for enlightenment.

Chang'an city, Tang dynasty

However, their stay in Chang'an was destined to be short-lived. The Buddhist deities, recognizing the successful completion of the mission, summoned the pilgrims for an audience with the Tathagata Buddha. In the divine presence, Tathagata expressed gratitude to the pilgrims for their dedication and bestowed upon them saintly positions within the Buddhist pantheon.

Tripitaka, the humble monk who had embarked on the pilgrimage, and Monkey, the irrepressible and loyal companion, were elevated to the esteemed status of Buddhas. Their merit in the arduous journey had not only secured the sacred scriptures but had also earned them the highest honor in the realm of enlightenment.

The pilgrims leave the Tang empire to become saints in the Western Heaven

As the celestial decree echoed through the heavens, the pilgrims basked in the radiant glow of divine recognition. The journey to the west, fraught with trials and tribulations, had culminated in a moment of transcendence. The pilgrims, now immortalized in the annals of Buddhist lore, stood as living embodiments of perseverance, wisdom, and the boundless potential for enlightenment.

Here ends The Journey to the West.

Published in the 16th century during the late Ming dynasty, Wu Cheng'en's defining novel Journey to the West built upon oral traditions and folk tales to become one of the Four Great Classical Novels of Chinese literature. It deeply impacted language, storytelling, religious metaphor, and the cultural landscape across China and wider Asian regions over the subsequent centuries until today.

The epic novel is considered a cornerstone of the classical Chinese novel tradition, pairing spiritual symbolism from Buddhism and Daoism with romantic fantasy and accounts of actual 7-8th century monk Xuanzang's pilgrimage. Its nonlinear structure in 100 chapters provides both overarching narrative and self-contained episodic adventures.

Many common Chinese idioms and phrases were derived from the novel's colorful depictions. Core characters like the Monkey King and Pigsy are ingrained cultural archetypes recognizable to most Asians. Opera, plays, stories, and films featuring these now beloved figures and their mythical exploits are continually produced across Greater

China, Japan, Korea and Southeast Asia - even inspiring some Hindu versions in regions exposed to Chinese diaspora.

The novel's themes balancing chaos and order through good-natured comic satire of human folly resonate through the ages and mediums. 500 years since first woodblock printed circulation, it remains among the most readable, enjoyable, insightful and beautifully penned works of Chinese fiction - cementing its cultural legacy across Asia for millennia to come.

As one of the four great classical Chinese novels, Journey to the West stands out for masterfully blending mythology, adventure, comedy, social commentary, and spiritual symbolism into a unified work of creativity and profound insight. Its literary excellence established the novel as a respected art form in China and inspired countless authors in the centuries since.

The novel insightfully examines the interplay between free will and fate, defiance and faith, animal impulse and higher wisdom – capturing timeless truths about human nature through the colorful characters of Monkey King, Tripitaka and others. Their fantastic escapades entertain imaginations of all ages while subtly conveying meaningful life lessons.

It adeptly balances comedy and drama without lodging wholly in satirical cynicism or moralistic preaching. Different readers across eras uncover fresh perspectives from its multidimensional portrayal of reality. The story rewards rereading for its psychological depth despite seeming like fanciful escapism on the surface.

Few works pack as much symbolic density encoded within adventures and ordeals into such lyrical poetic prose in just 100 chapters. These factors contribute to Journey to the West remaining a seminal pillar of both Chinese and global literary heritage nearly 500 years after its first publication at the close of the Ming dynasty. The novel's beautiful writing, meaningful messages and rich inspirations shall endure for centuries more.

Endnotes

As we reach the conclusion of this exploration into the mythical realms of *Journey to the West*, we extend our gratitude to all who have accompanied us on this enlightening journey. Wu Cheng'en's masterpiece has stood the test of time, weaving tales that transcend cultural boundaries and continue to captivate hearts around the world.

This journey has not been solitary, for we've treaded alongside the indomitable Monkey King, Sun Wukong, and his companions – Tripitaka, Pigsy, and Sandy – through trials, encounters with demons and deities, and profound moral lessons.

Black Myth: Wukong emerges as a contemporary expression of this timeless tale, a video game that breathes new life into the narrative. Game Science Studio's ambitious endeavor to bring the Monkey King's adventures to life speaks to the enduring appeal of this classic.

As of the current writing in December 2023, the details surrounding the story of Black Myth: Wukong remain largely shrouded in mystery. Therefore, this book might not delve into some potentially crucial aspects of the game's narrative that may emerge in the future. However, we anticipate the opportunity to enhance and expand upon this book as more information becomes available about this highly anticipated game. Our commitment is to keep readers informed and provide a comprehensive understanding of Black Myth: Wukong as soon as we gain access to additional details about this exciting and upcoming gaming experience. Stay tuned for future reversions and enrichments to ensure you receive the most comprehensive insights into the unfolding story of the game.

Our aim has been to serve as a cultural bridge, ensuring that Western audiences fully appreciate the depth and richness of Journey to the West. The landscapes envisioned in the game, the characters' moral journeys, and the cultural context that birthed this masterpiece are all facets we've explored together.

Whether you are a seasoned scholar of world literature or a newcomer to the fantastical realms of Sun Wukong, we hope this book has been your guide, offering insights and unlocking the gates to the magical world of Journey to the West. As you embark on your own odyssey, may the pages of this classic and the immersive experience of Black Myth: Wukong continue to enchant and enlighten.

Our appreciation extends to the creators, scholars, and enthusiasts who keep the spirit of Journey to the West alive, ensuring its enduring legacy in the hearts and minds of generations to come. May the magic of this tale continue to resonate, transcending time and culture, inviting all to partake in the wondrous odyssey of Sun Wukong and his companions.